AF428030

Never One Without the Other

SERGIO VILLANUEVA

MILTON & HUGO L.L.C.
1001 3rd Avenue West,
Suite 430 Bradenton,
FL 34205, USA

Website: www. miltonandhugo.com
Hotline: 1- 888-778-0033
Email: info@miltonandhugo.com

Ordering Information:
Quantity sales. Special discounts are available on quantity purchases by corporations, associations, and others. For details, contact the publisher at the address above.

ISBN-13:   979-8-89285-799-4   [Paperback Edition]
               979-8-89285-800-7   [Hardback Edition]
               979-8-89285-798-7   [Digital Edition]

Rev. date: 03/03/2026

Never One Without the Other

SERGIO VILLANUEVA

Once there was a forest in the sky, full of life and trees. The forest was very special – it had a one of a kind black deer. This deer was indeed special. It was also immortal. It had lived a long life, so long that it had bare witness of many generations of species. An odd thing to say for that this deer was also blind.

Many animals called it a saint; others called him wise. He always stayed under an oak tree. Animals of many kinds visited the deer for advice, including the plants. They asked the deer many things: where to hunt, where to grown, where to spread its seeds. In return, the deer asked for nothing.

any years have kept passing, and then came a small rose. For a while, many animals and plants admired the rose. Unlike the others, it was white. It was beautiful, too. Then, a day has passed when someone decided to take care of this rose and plucked it from its roots. Days with the plant they took care of it, but soon, it neglected the rose's needs. It neglected small requests from the rose and left it behind. The rose is now wilting, its petals now falling. What was once a beautiful rose now became a wilting distress. It cried, but no answers, for that the plants that also loved the rose, neglected it as well. Surrounding itself with its fine full of thorns, she cut herself off from everyone else in order to protect herself from everyone.

year has passed since then. The deer remained under the oak tree giving advice. Before all of a sudden, one morning, her rose, standing tall, he headed towards the rose as if drawn to it. He laid next to the white rose surrounded by its thorny bush, and then he spoke.

Black Deer: *"You seem to be in distress."*

The white rose, not noticing the deer at first, surprised the rose a bit but decided to respond.

White Rose: *"I'm fine."*

The black deer, though blind, still managed to go face towards the rose.

Black Deer: *"You don't sound like you are."*

The white rose has never heard of this black deer before, unaware of what he is. It decided to continue the conversation.

White Rose: *"Well, if you can't tell, I'm wilting, I'm irritable."*

The deer only made a small laugh.

Black Deer: *"Well, I cannot tell, for I am blind. But you sound beautiful."*

The rose turned to the black deer confused on what he just said.

he white rose became curious.

White Rose: *"How can you say something like that? You don't even know what I look like. You're blind."*

The deer only smiled once again.

Black Deer: *"You may be right, but I bet you were once the most beautiful there was."*

The white rose was astonished how he could have known this.

White Rose: *"You are correct. How did you know this?"*

The black deer responded.

Black Deer: *"You surround yourself in your vines of thorns. You say you are wilting. You must have had some pain and negligence so you closed yourself off to no longer feel such pain."*

The white rose stayed silent before saying something.

White Rose: *"Is it that obvious?"*

The black deer merely nodded. The white rose then quickly turned to the deer.

White Rose: *"Wait, how do you know about my thorn vines?"*

The black deer slowly turned to the sound of the white rose's voice.

Black Deer: *"Because I stepped on one when lying down."*

The white rose quickly apologized. But the deer refused her apology.

Black Deer: *"Don't be sorry, I just wasn't paying attention."*

The white rose was very surprised by this but very relieved – she hadn't been in a while.

For the next fews days, the deer took care of the rose. Despite the rose insisiting not to. At one point, the rose compared the black deer to a husky fow how stubborn he was. As time passed, the rose opened up to the deer. Her thorns moved away but still remained. The deer explained what he was and impressed the rose. It has been a while since the deer enjoyed himself in any way. He loved the white rose's company. He told a story while being with the rose. The rose loved to listen. Every now and then, a sheep would come by and listen as well bringing along stuff like axes and knives. The deer and rose never questioned it. Then it was time. The deer turned to the rose.

Black Deer: *"I would like to show you to the world. No longer shall we stay in the dense forest."*

The rose quickly exclaimed, not wanting to reveal herself.

he rose, afraid of not having dirt, was reassured by the black deer, allowing her to use his immortality to be sapped by her. In return, the black deer was able to see again. He saw the light once more. Carrying the rose, they both headed towards a pond. From there, he looked down into the water and stared at their reflection. He made a soft smile before speaking.

Black Deer: *"I told you, you looked beautiful."*

The white rose was staring at her reflection. Not only was she blooming again, but she was better than before she was wilting. She was the most beautiful flower. The white rose thanked the black deer. From this moment forward, they both relied on each other. The white rose needed the immortality of the deer and the deer needed the rose to see. Both became never one without the other.

As time passed, animals still came by the oak tree to see the deer and admire the beautiful white rose. The deer grew older while the white rose still looked beautiful. The deer, being able to age thanks to the rose, slowly died. Then soon, the white rose – both accepting being together to the end. Once the rose released her seeds, they began to grow on the deer making both beautiful white and black roses surrounding the oak tree. Once in a while, the same sheep came by and told their story to new animals.

egend says that if you were to go near the tree and listen to the black and white roses, it'll tell you the things you need to know.

FIN